Dear Parent:
Your child's love of reading starts here!

Every child learns to read in a different way and at his or her own speed. Some go back and forth between reading levels and read favorite books again and again. Others read through each level in order. You can help your young reader improve and become more confident by encouraging his or her own interests and abilities. From books your child reads with you to the first books he or she reads alone, there are I Can Read Books for every stage of reading:

SHARED READING
Basic language, word repetition, and whimsical illustrations, ideal for sharing with your emergent reader

BEGINNING READING
Short sentences, familiar words, and simple concepts for children eager to read on their own

READING WITH HELP
Engaging stories, longer sentences, and language play for developing readers

READING ALONE
Complex plots, challenging vocabulary, and high-interest topics for the independent reader

ADVANCED READING
Short paragraphs, chapters, and exciting themes for the perfect bridge to chapter books

I Can Read Books have introduced children to the joy of reading since 1957. Featuring award-winning authors and illustrators and a fabulous cast of beloved characters, I Can Read Books set the standard for beginning readers.

A lifetime of discovery begins with the magical words **"I Can Read!"**

Visit www.icanread.com for information
on enriching your child's reading experience.

I Can Read Book® is a trademark of HarperCollins Publishers.

The Berenstain Bears Take Off! Copyright © 2016 by Berenstain Publishing, Inc. All rights reserved. Manufactured in U.S.A. No part of this book may be used or reproduced in any manner whatsoever without written permission except in the case of brief quotations embodied in critical articles and reviews. For information address HarperCollins Children's Books, a division of HarperCollins Publishers, 195 Broadway, New York, NY 10007.
www.icanread.com

Library of Congress Control Number: 2015947482
ISBN 978-0-06-235019-0 (trade bdg.) — ISBN 978-0-06-235018-3 (pbk.)

16 17 18 19 20 LSCC   10 9 8 7 6 5 4 3
❖
First Edition

I Can Read!™

BEGINNING READING 1

The Berenstain Bears®

TAKE OFF!

AIR SHOW TOURS

Mike Berenstain
Based on the characters created by
Stan and Jan Berenstain

HARPER

An Imprint of HarperCollinsPublishers

"Look!" says Brother Bear.

"There is an air show today!"

"Let's go!" says Sister Bear.

"Good idea," says Papa.

"It'll be fun," says Mama.

"Plane!" says Honey. "Zoom! Zoom!"

"That is the first plane that ever flew," says Mama.

"It doesn't fly very high," says Sister.

"Or very far!" says Brother.

"But it *does* fly," says Papa.

"More planes were soon built," says Papa.

"They flew higher, faster, and farther."

"There are so many different kinds!"
says Mama.

"That one is long and skinny," says
Brother.

"This one has its tail in the front," says
Sister.

"Let's go up in a balloon!" says Mama.

"Welcome!" says the guide.

"You can see the show from the air."

"What a view!" says Papa.

"Tell us all about the planes," says Mama.

11

"These are old fighter planes," says the guide.

"They were early planes used in war."

"That one has two wings," says Brother.

"This one has three wings," says Sister.

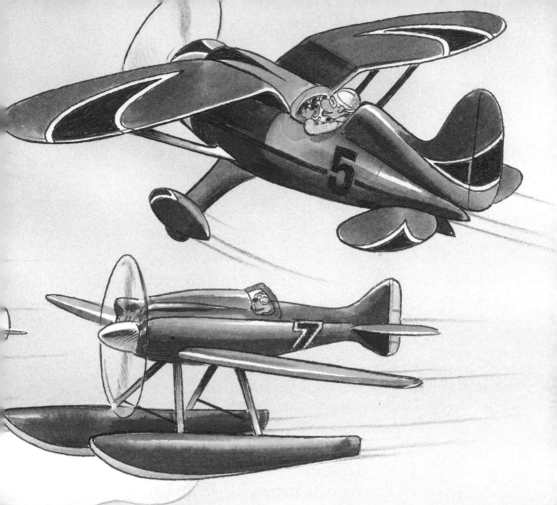

"Wow!" says Papa. "Those planes are
fast!"

"They had to be," says the guide.

"They're racing planes.

And the fastest plane won the race."

"Those planes are sort of slow," says Brother.

"Not all planes need to go fast," says the guide.

"Some planes are like your family car. They just need to get from here to there."

"Look at those planes go!" says Brother.

"That doesn't look safe," says Mama.

"It wasn't," says the guide.

"These are warplanes.

That's how they flew in a big fight."

"Those planes are loud!" says Sister.

"And big!" says Papa.

"They're giant warplanes," says the guide.

"They were called flying forts."

"They sound strong," says Mama.

"Roar! Roar!" says Honey.

"Some big planes are for travel," says the

guide.

"This jumbo jet will take you on a trip.

It can fly across the sea.

It will take you to faraway lands."

"Jet planes can fly very fast," says the guide.

"Some have strange shapes."

"This one has a pointy nose," says Brother.

"That one looks like a big bat," says Sister.

"This is a rocket plane," says the guide.

"It flew faster than any plane before it."

"Whoosh!" says Honey.

"Not all aircraft have wings,"

says the guide.

"A blimp is lighter than air."

"Like our balloon?" asks Sister.

"Yes," says the guide.

"But a blimp uses a motor to fly."

"Helicopters also fly without wings," says the guide.

"Spinning blades keep them up."

"They make a chopping sound," says Mama.

"That's why they're called choppers," says the guide.

"Chop! Chop! Chop!" says Honey.

"Some planes can fly without power," says the guide.

"They sail on the wind for miles and miles.

"Some planes are very small,"
says the guide.
"You can build an ultralight
yourself."
"Putt! Putt! Putt!" says Honey.

"Thank you for the tour," says Papa.

"Look! I'm a plane!" says Brother.

"Me too!" says Sister.

"Now we have our own air show!"
says Mama.

"Brrm! Brrm!" says Honey.